Bobby Johnston's book is much more than a coming-of-age memoir: It's an intimate portrait of a group of Rust Belt misfits and the community they've built, with all its wonders and secrets, its transcendent moments, and its horrors. Johnston plays so many different emotional notes in this collection: his stories are funny and haunting; tender and violent; realistic and psychedelic. *The Saint I Ain't* is a moving and finely-crafted work of literary art.
— Héctor Tobar, Pulitzer Prize-winner and author of New York Times bestseller, *Deep Down Dark*

Bobby Johnston has written what amounts to a novel length poem, both drenched in the bawdy and colorful language of a saloon storyteller as well as the sublime prose and story engine of the best coming of age novels. A treat to be devoured in one sitting, or better yet, read aloud over a glass or three of your favorite tipple. A wondrous and wonderful debut.
— Scott Frank, Oscar and Emmy nominated screenwriter/director of *The Queen's Gambit* and author of the novel *Shaker*

In *The Saint I Ain't*, writer and musician Bobby Johnston has given us an entire portfolio of snapshots from a vexatious childhood, as vivid as if they'd been taken an hour ago, still wet from the bath of memory.
— Jim Krusoe, author of *The Sleep Garden*

The Saint I Ain't is a lovely set of narrative poems about a catholic boy growing up somewhere in the wilds of the blue collar seventies. Filled both with peculiar, vivid details and a spare economy of language, it is a rare treat. Calling to mind both Denis Johnson's *Jesus' Son* and Dylan Thomas' *A Child's Christmas in Wales*, it is both sweet and dark with a wonderfully understated delivery that asks you to look into the abyss for yourself.
— PT Elliott, author of *The Sociopath's Guide to Getting Ahead*

The Saint I Ain't

Stories from Sycamore Street

Bobby Johnston

Fomite
Burlington, VT

ISBN-13: 978-1-947917-75-0
Library of Congress Control Number: 2020941987
Fomite
58 Peru Street
Burlington, VT 05401

"there is but one truly serious philosophical problem,
and that is suicide.
judging whether life is or is not worth living
amounts to answering the fundamental question of philosophy"
– albert camus

contents

sycamore street   1

bitten   3

baldy   5

only the lonely   9

father ferguson   13

harmonica joe   17

me and mr. t   19

the saint i ain't   23

the long arm   29

and also with you   33

sweet sympathy   39

the ohio blue tip   45

rat of the land   49

sister vincent   55

batter up   61

buddy   67

seventh heaven   71

ten in the clip   79

ben   83

fireball   87

one for the road   93

the island   97

clegy for me   103

sycamore street

when i walked out the front door
of the house i grew up in,
i saw undergarments drying in the wind.
but not swaying.
they were motion-resistant, tempered fortresses
designed to cloak rather than cling.
they were worn by god's wives,
sisters of mercy,
NUNS.

i felt i was surely damned
for the passive misfortune
of living in a house that faced uphill,
directly toward the back balcony of
saint agnes convent.

next door was saint agnes grammar school, where i was
sentenced to serve kindergarten through eighth grade.
you may know people who went to other schools,
sharing classes with bruce springsteen or stevie nicks,
but saint agnes produced
assailants, school shooters
and suicides.

next to the school,
across a narrow, brick road
was saint agnes church.

it was an immense, stone continent
with three stories of stained glass
and the school cafeteria in the basement.

the block of the church was shared with
the rectory, where priests lived
and the home of the church organist
where i took piano lessons.

the south side of sycamore street was inhabited
by a handful of drowning families
that were flailing in quicksand.

one of those families was mine...

bitten

i've been bitten.
sometimes i asked for it.

when i was around seven years old,
badger farley told his mother
that i bit him.
to this day i'm not sure that i did,
but i'm pretty sure.

badger's mother ordered me into their backyard.
it had the artificial-turf look
of the brady bunch backyard.
but badger's mother was no carol.

she rolled up my left sleeve,
clamped my wrist
and pulled my arm straight.

then she bit into my upper arm
with the purging fervor of a baptist minister.
she held long and hard.
her temples pulsed,
her head shook,
and she released.

she studied her work.

she even seemed satisfied.
but without breaking her focus from my arm,
she said, "ruby."

ruby was badger's sister.
she squared off and nodded
as her mother pointed to my arm.

i had always told her that she looked like miss piggy.
but she bit like her mother.

after she released, she stuck her tongue out at me.

badger's mother called him by his birth name,
"leonard".
leonard looked at the ground as he took position.
he bit quickly and without passion.

this was partly because he had no top teeth,
but mostly because he knew
that neither one of us was going anywhere
and he was the only kid on the south side
who was smaller than me.

baldy

baldy was older than death.
he was nocturnal,
maybe even a vampire.

to the 8 year-old mind
only one thing was certain;
baldy was dangerous.

on rare occasions, there were actual sightings of baldy.

baldy was a hairless, mobile fossil
who wore a cold grimace, black clothing
and always carried a shovel.
the older kids called him
a murderer, mortician,
grave digger.

these weren't campfire-quality ghost stories
told over orange sodas in backyard tents.

they were possible fates.
threat fuel.
the death sentence for young kids
who would not bow to neighborhood bullies.

lewis gurston was too large for his size.
i was tiny, but loud.
written in bold print.

he didn't miss me,
or the opportunity.

lewis slapped one handcuff onto my left wrist.
he used the attached cuff to pull me through the meadow
behind our houses
until
we reached baldy's backyard.
it was long, narrow and ominously well kept.
each side was bordered with a perfectly symmetrical row
of thin, weeping trees.

he told me the trees were grave markers.
then he handcuffed me to one in the middle,
turned, cupped his hands over his mouth
and screamed,
"fuck you baldy"!!!
"you piece of shit"!!!

i wasn't waiting to die.
like a frantic, trapped animal i turned and clawed repeatedly
at my wrist, the handcuffs and the tree branch.
my skin was torn raw.
i thought in fast, red flashes about baldy,
the shovel and being buried alive.
i collapsed, sobbing.

after a slow century of moments
i opened one eye.
finally,
i turned around.

baldy hadn't come for me.

lewis gurston hadn't left.

he wasn't even laughing.
i'm not even sure he enjoyed it.

as he released me,
he said he knew baldy was away that weekend,
and next time
i wouldn't be so lucky.

i don't remember ever seeing baldy again.

only the lonely

it all began
with the underwear and bra sections
of my mother's department store catalogs.
but soon
my sights were set
on the housewife next door
and my second grade teacher.

this was long before i knew
that a grown woman deserved
the common courtesy of being able
to bend over
without some adolescent hefner looking down her top.

you see,
i was fortunate to have my early childhood
coincide with the "rising" popularity of the mini–skirt.

because of this wonderful convergence of time and space,
my favorite activity became sitting under the kitchen table
while looking up my baby-sitters' skirts
as they chatted with their boyfriends on the telephone.

my peeping tom days
reached a peak
on the day of my uncle's second wedding.

that night,
my uncle and his beautiful, young bride
(in her beautiful, low-cut dress)
came to my parents' house to open wedding presents.

i advantageously positioned myself behind her,
sitting on the back of the couch.

i realized from that angle the adults
would think i was looking over her shoulder
at their generous gifts,
rather than hers.

all of this
is not to say
that i was completely dismissive
of girls my own age.

in fact,
i once cast myself opposite rosetta lando
in my original production of
"KISSING FOR THE NEIGHBORHOOD KIDS."

but instead of the rave reviews i had expected,
it garnished reprimands from our parents,
and me being perceived as "gross" by the girls
and a "sissy" by the boys.

it was just as well;
i thought girls my age looked too much like boys anyway,
and the boys i knew
were playground-strutting, upright apes.

besides,
i truly felt it was only a matter of time
before some full-grown,
fully developed juliet
would see me for all i had to offer.

when i was nine years old,
i believed my time had come
when my parents hired
miranda henley to baby-sit.

miranda henley was the most beautiful
high school girl in our neighborhood
and i had a HUGE crush on her.

but the best thing
was that she always called me her "boyfriend"
(of course, this was only because i was small and "cute"...
still, i couldn't help believing her).

ever the optimist,
i planned the evening as if it were a real "date".

my idea was to wow her with my father's record collection,
and then let nature take its course.

so, while my siblings were outside
milking their last bit of playtime
before being called in for bed,
i sat miranda down on the couch to
"show her some cool music."

for the first cut
i chose a sure thing:
roy orbison's sultry, pleading
"only the lonely".

when roy's quivering, falsetto pipes
faded with the end of the song,
i turned to miranda
to see if she was as moved as i was.

unimpressed,
she chuckled and said that roy orbison
wasn't exactly her idea of "cool" music.

then she told me to go upstairs
and brush my teeth.

father ferguson

in our town
there was no separation of church and state.
or of church and fate.

one way or another
they got their hands on you.

for me, the hands
belonged to father ferguson;
an underestimated,
overgrown, catholic priest
at saint agnes church.

he was a friend of my father
who was trusted to baby-sit
when i was a young boy.

father ferguson was an eerily solemn,
six-and-a-half-foot mountain
whose lurking presence
was given away by his breathing...
which was loud and through his nose.

his thick stare
was projected through
the coke—bottle lenses
of his black framed glasses.

this magnified his eyes
to a disturbing proportion.

for years, father ferguson hid behind
the assumed virtue
of his white collar.
but eventually,
his cover would be blown,
exposing a web of abuse.

the catholic diocese
treated the father ferguson situation
as an exception, rather than the rule.

they vowed to deal with it firmly,
but discreetly.

father ferguson disappeared
under the dark wing of catholicism...

years later,
when i was in sixth grade,
our class walked in two lines
across the narrow brick road
between the school and the church.

we were going to confession.
when it was my turn to confess,
i stepped into the dark, wooden booth.

as soon as i knelt down
i recognized the nasal breathing
and saw father ferguson's
silhouette behind the thick screen.

i gasped in panic.

then i swallowed,
and began to speak
the confessional script
slowly,
and so quietly
i could barely hear myself.

"bless me father for i have sinned.
it's been two weeks since my last confession."

he didn't respond.
my ears burned
and my eyelids began to bulge.

i couldn't say another word.

that day,
father ferguson
assigned me no penance
for my sins.

harmonica joe

harmonica joe hid inside a snowmobile suit.
whether it was summer or winter didn't matter.
he was a turtle.

his shell was dark blue with three dingy, white stripes
running down each sleeve.

as far as i could tell,
he only used three of many available pockets.
one was for the rag he used as a handkerchief
and the other two were for carrying harmonicas;
both in the key of C.

harmonica joe only played in the key of C
and he only played "when the saints go marching in".

he walked down sycamore street once a week.
the only thing that would break his
strolling gaze from the sidewalk
was the request for a song.
he always agreed
and would immediately begin tapping the insole
of his right foot against the concrete in a reckless meter.

he would pull out a C harmonica
and beat it against the leg of his snowmobile suit
to remove spit and particles from the last performance.

without looking into your eyes, he would say,
"here's one you're gonna like,"
then he would proceed into
"when the saints go marching in".

no matter what song was requested,
it was followed by a nod of affirmation
and his trademark statement and song.
this imaginary conversion
was completed with a harmonica change,
giving the impression of a change of keys.

once, during a party at our house,
my father invited harmonica joe inside
to entertain his friends.
it was a comedy billed as a music show,
generating knowing winks and condescending praise.

after the show,
i followed my father and joe into the kitchen,
where my father gave him a piece of cake.

he didn't want anyone getting the wrong impression.
or the right one.

i formed my own impressions regardless:

my father liked easy comparisons.
harmonica joe liked cake,
and i liked the idea of compensating
the fool.

i am currently a professional musician.

me and mr. t

my mother said she knew
i was going to be a musician
from the beginning.

when i was 14 months old
she came into the living room
to find me pulling myself
to the top of our old upright piano
while standing on the keyboard.

she believed it was an omen.

by the time i was 4 years old
i was playing by ear,
picking out music from shows i'd seen on television.

i spent hours at that piano,
every day for years.
i made up original pieces,
played television themes,
or just let my favorite chords
sustain while tilting my ear toward the aging wood.

i actually took lessons for about five years,
but was never interested in learning about technique
or reading music.
my relationship with the piano
was about escape, rather than mastery.

my debut concert
was for my father's drinking buddies;
i performed in the living room
while they played cards in the kitchen.

the repertoire consisted of originals and t.v. themes
like "hill street blues",
"the young and the restless"
and "brian's song".

each piece ended with encouraging yelps from the kitchen
and an occasional quarter or two.

it was the first time
i knew my father was proud of me.

my first gig outside the living room
was when i was fourteen years old.
my band played a dance at the public junior high school.

after the first set
i walked into the back hallway
and was met by a couple dozen gushing girls.

one girl handed me her gold necklace
and asked if i would wear it during the second set.

as i tried to fit it over my suddenly inflated head,
the other girls began to ask if i would also
wear their necklaces.

when we took the stage for the second set,
i must have looked like an eighty-pound tom jones
doing his mr. t impression.

but i didn't care.

my oldest friend; music,
had suddenly shown me
some very new possibilities.

the saint i ain't

my relationship
with the nuns who taught
and tyrannized us
at saint agnes school,
went downhill from day one
of first grade.

but i swear it was entrapment...

for kindergarten
they gave us mrs. daley,
a "civilian" teacher.

she was a warm, safe, grandmother hug
that lasted all year.

in mrs. daley's class
we all grew tender and soft:
30 fresh, trusting, hansels and gretels
ready to be served up
to first grade,
and sister mary vivian.

my first move
on the first day
of first grade
was to hide in the bathroom
under the pretense of a "BM".

during my self-exile,
a fellow student began knocking on the door
with her own requests to use the bathroom.

these requests continued with increased urgency
until the holy one herself
came to the door,
screaming and ordering me to give up
control of the headquarters.

i eventually came out,
defeated.

foiled by one of my own.

i turned to glare at the other student
and saw the puddle under her chair.

my glare had barely faded
when her holiness grabbed me by the hair
and dragged me to the principal's office.

this was the inaugural
of my many journeys to see
sister gosilano;
the big one
in the big room.

sister gosilano
was an infinitely obese,
growling, dictator of a nun,
whose name sounded closer to
godzilla than it did to god.

she always received me as if i were
a painful, recurring rash
(indeed, the symptoms were there).

sister gosilano
and the other nuns at saint agnes
were of an order called the "sisters of mercy"
(a clear case of false advertising).

the sisters of mercy
drew their remedies from the old testament's
"an eye for an eye",
rather than jesus and his new testament of
turning the other cheek.

for example:
one day, some of us were spitting water
at other students.
a nun lined us up
beside the drinking fountain
and repeatedly spat in our faces
at point-blank range.

and then,
when my friend billy flynn
put a tack on a girl's chair,
a nun put three tacks on his chair
and forced him down onto them,
pushing him by the shoulders.

these punishments appear docile
next to the consequences they rendered
for more serious offenses.

for me,
saint agnes would become
a lopsided, eight year battle.

i was david,
they were goliath,
and i was choosing my stone...

whether by freewill or predestination,
i found it one day,
while loitering in the third floor hallway.

i looked down the stairwell,
through three floors of descending staircase
to see three nuns talking
in the school basement
right beneath me.
sister gosilano's hulking figure was in the middle.

i rubbed my hands together
as i let the saliva build up in my bottom lip
until it almost poured out.
when i could no longer hold it,
i released.
perhaps i actually giggled out loud,
or maybe she could sense the impending evil,
but in slow motion,
sister gosilano looked up and caught my eyes
as the spit was in mid-flight.

i pulled my head back from the stairway
and stood frozen.

a guttural growl
rose up the stairwell,
shaking my skeleton loose from its tendons.
the only words i could make out
were my name
and something about being expelled.

for a moment
i waited
as my heart raced.

without making a conscious decision,
i turned, slid down three railings in a row
and burst out the back door of the school.

i ran to my house
and hid beneath the stairs
in the basement,
until my father came home.

the long arm

in our house, my father was the law
and i was the criminal.

i spent my entire childhood
suspected, pursued, apprehended,
and punished.

although my father sometimes used excessive force,
he felt the payoff would be worth the pain.

after these instances
he would send me to my room,
where i would lie on the bed,
scraping varnish off the headboard
with my bottom teeth.

eventually, he would knock on the door of my room.

he'd come in
and sit at the edge of my bed,
telling me how difficult some things were
and how much he loved me.

once, during a
passionate pursuit,
i was trying to escape up the stairs
when my father caught me halfway.

he grabbed onto one ankle
and pulled my legs out from under me,
forcing my face into the stairs.

i broke free and continued climbing
only to have him
knock me down again
with a kick to my backside.
he got me once more,
swinging sidearm,
before i scrambled into my room.

my head was throbbing.

after a while,
i opened my bedroom door
and looked into the upstairs hallway
to make sure the coast was clear.
then i went into the bathroom to inspect my wounds.

when i looked in the mirror
i was disappointed to see
there was only a small bruise on my cheekbone
as evidence of the altercation.

i became enraged
and began punching myself on the cheek,
right where the tiny bruise was.

once it started swelling,
i pulled open a paper clip
and dug into the skin
until i had produced some bleeding.

when the horror
of my face was satisfactory,
i went downstairs
to make my father see
what he had done to me.

my father was in his chair
reading the newspaper.

when i walked up and stopped in front of him,
he put the paper down
and looked at me without saying anything.
i could see his eyes focusing on my cheek.

after a moment,
he picked up his paper again
and opened it between us.

from behind the newspaper
he told me
that my injuries appeared to be
self-inflicted.

and also with you

when i was in fifth grade
i landed the best gig
a catholic kid could get;
being an altar boy.

especially for weddings,
baptisms, and funerals.

these were the three types of masses
that involved tips for the altar boys.

they formed the holy trinity of the altar boy racket.

catholics were efficient
if nothing else.
whether you were coming or going
there was a lineup of people taking their piece...
and mine was usually about 5 bucks.

weddings and baptisms
were inconsistent at best.
their payoff depended upon the generosity
of the happy families
(good luck).

which brings us back again,
to the funeral.
and funeral homes that made lots of money.

they were run by businessmen
who tipped altar boys
to assure punctuality and servitude
(although some paid better than others).

but,
beyond the money,
the eucharist wars (they fly!),
the stolen swigs of altar wine and mock confessions,
the best part about being an altar boy
was definitely
getting out of class at saint agnes prison.

again, this was mostly for funerals
(weddings and baptisms were weekend events).

naturally, we took our job seriously,
checking the obituaries to see which
funeral home was handling the duties
and verifying which classes we would miss.

all that was left
was to pad our schedule
by swapping dates with altar boys
who didn't have a system down yet.

although this was a life on easy street,
the temptation for mischief
would often be too much
and i did things to put my job in peril...

sometimes masses were performed by
priests from other parishes,
providing a sense of anonymity among the ranks.

one such mass was performed
by an old, irish leprechaun of a priest
who called us "laddie" and laughed with his mouth wide open.

it almost seemed too easy...

during the apex of the service
my brother and i,
with our co-conspirators, the flynn brothers,
broke into our "make each other
laugh during mass" routine.

we were flanking the altar
in pairs, kneeling.

"father o'reverend"
was on the altar, blessing the eucharist and wine.

next, when he held them up above his head,
i was to ring the silver hand bell
on the little green square of carpet next to me.

when "o'reverend" held up the eucharist
and my moment had come,
in my head
i heard a circus drum roll
rather than a soft bell ringing.

i raised the bell by the handle
and gave it an obnoxiously loud, sustained ringing.

the old priest didn't even flinch.

there was only a muffled snicker
and a fake cough from my fellow altar boys.

undaunted, i put my hand on the bell and waited
for the raising of the wine.

"o'reverend" put both hands on the chalice and lifted.

i picked up the bell again,
and this time
let loose with a thunderous ringing
that must have reached all the way to god,
because in mid-ring, the bell flew out of my hand
and cleared the altar in a loping arc.

it hit the floor
in front of the altar
and omitted a series of dying pings
as it awkwardly rolled to a stop.

i stared at the bell.
there was no sound for what seemed like eternity,
and then i turned to look at the old priest.

he was staring at me,
blankly,
over the top of his spectacles.

after a moment,
he shook his head disappointedly
and continued mass.

i performed the remainder of my duties
as if i were walking down death row.

after mass,
my brother and the flynns left the
altar boy chambers with haste
and i waited for the wrath of god.

when the old, irish priest eventually came in,
he walked over to me
and bent down to my eye level.

i could feel my leg twitching
as i braced myself.
then, very sweetly,
much like a grandpa,
he said,
"i think you're ringing too hard laddie,
it just needs a little tinkle."

my fear collapsed
and i broke into a giant smile.

"yes father."

sweet sympathy

i had a high-impact
childhood.

our neighbor,
mr. hinkley used to joke
that if i lived to be
twelve years old,
i'd make it to one hundred.

my laundry list
of accidents and injuries
would have filled a medical journal.

but, even with a solid foundation,
rooted in the classics
(cracked teeth, broken fingers and toes,
fractured collarbone, broken foot,
splintered elbow,
and a nose that had been reshaped
more times than an amateur boxer's),
i still found new, inventive ways
of attracting trauma.

there was the time i ran, arms extended
through the plate glass
of our front door,
leaving my hands bleeding as if they'd
been thrust into a bucket of ginsu knives.

another time,
billy flynn and i
attempted to surprise mr. hinkley
by removing a tree stump
from his backyard.
this ended with billy's first swing of the axe,
which completely missed the stump,
yet struck squarely
against my skull.

but, my pièce de résistance
had to be the morning i tripped
while running with a hollow tentpole.

i defied the odds
of both physics and chance
by landing with the aluminum pipe
going straight into my mouth,
lacerating my throat and slicing off
half of my uvula
(never to be seen again).

this sent me
bolting toward the house,
screaming and spewing blood
like a pint-sized gene simmons.

these catastrophes were
routinely sprung upon my dauntless mother,
who was adept at applying
critical first-aid and
unsurprisingly,
would later become a nurse-practitioner.

but, being poor in the 1970s
meant that very few injuries
resulted in a doctor's visit.
and even less in a trip to the hospital.

my father's patent response
to statements like
"my arm hurts when i move it like this",
was to say
"don't move your arm like that".

he had little tolerance
for garden-variety maladies
since my older brother had already
been through a half dozen surgeries
for birth anomalies
by the time he was five years old
(with many more to follow).

i spent countless weeks
of my adolescence
at my grandparents' house
while my mother and father accompanied
my brother to the big city,
where he underwent
painful and traumatizing procedures.

but, what i noticed most about the experience,
was the outpouring of love and support
he received from friends and family.

there were balloons, cards,
stuffed animals and
the kind of receptive embrace
that a trouble-making kid like me could
only dream of.

i had vivid fantasies
about the girls from st. agnes grammar school
visiting me on my deathbed,
distraught over the fact that they
had overlooked me for so many years.

every time i had a medical emergency
i wondered if it was finally going to be
the BIG one.

my second concussion
would ultimately be the event
that landed me in the hospital
for an overnight stay
(likely because i had projectile vomited
all over my desk during science class).

once i was settled in my room,
i asked if we could call my brother
to let him know where i was.

my brother was appropriately unimpressed.
especially when he heard the concussion
was caused by losing my grip
while swinging from the pipes in the boys bathroom
and landing on the concrete floor.

he said nobody was going to come visit me
just for being an idiot.

the next morning
i woke up with a massive, throbbing headache
and debilitating nausea.

but alas,
no balloons, cards, stuffed animals,
or sweet sympathy.

the ohio blue tip

looking back,
i think the little rascals
were to blame.

particularly the episode
where they played "hooky"
and went fishing
to escape the dull torture of school.

being ten years old,
i missed the moral message at the end
about how truancy doesn't pay.

instead, i took away
a newly formed, bohemian belief
that school was for suckers.

on the playground,
it took about three minutes
to convince a few classmates that
our fleeting youth
would be better spent
fishing at the river
than wasting away in some
"nun-run" classroom
at saint agnes school.

the following day
we traded in our morning prayer and pledge of allegiance
for a few hours of mini-male bonding
near the bridge by my house.

we took great care
in bringing our best fishing poles
and complete tackle boxes.
for me, this meant
invading the forbidden realm of my father's fishing gear.

when we reached the river's edge
and dug into our tackle kits,
i was delighted to find
my father had stocked his with
a box of ohio blue tip matches,
which could be lit by striking against almost anything.

soon,
any concerns we had about
what bait to use
or which fish to catch,
gave way to the most primitive object
of human fascination:
fire.

first,
we put on a pyrotechnic show
by igniting matches on our front teeth, fingernails
and boot heels.

next,
we staged a rousing game of
"arsonists and firefighters".

for this, one of us faced the river
while throwing a lit match
back over his shoulder.

the others waited at the top of
the grass-covered dike
until it was nicely ignited,
then they rolled down through the flames,
extinguishing the fire
and proving their manhood.

as the game went on
we waited longer and longer
before putting out each fire.

this really wasn't such a big deal...

until the wind began to pick up.

as fate would have it,
i threw the final ohio blue tip
that turned the entire river bank into a raging inferno...

besides the ordeal that followed in the police station,
and being grounded for months,
the worst part of it all was looking out the car window
at the burnt stretch of dike
whenever my family drove across the bridge by our house.

every time we passed
my father would point at it
while looking in the opposite direction.

he called it my "autograph":

a patch of black earth
to go with my black cloud.

rat of the land

the lower animals didn't stand a chance
in the wake of my family's
manifest destiny.

they were often the first to go.

at some point,
my father got the idea
that the tiny red squirrels
at our hunting cabin in the woods
were aggressive toward the larger grays
(which were more desirable
as a hunting spoil).

he promised my older brother
twenty-five cents a head for
any red squirrel he shot,
and said i could assist.

so, my brother grabbed his .22
and the two of us got straight to work...

to keep track of our tally,
i would shout an updated head count to my father
as i tossed each new carcass onto the fire pit
that always seemed to be
burning behind the cabin.

to this day,
i get nauseous from the sensory memory
of singed animal fur.

eventually, my brother and i abandoned
our wholesale assault on red squirrels
when we found out
there was more money to be made
in the aquatic rodent market.

we learned
that the toxic, algae-filled streams
on the west end of town,
which seethed with glowing waste
from the remaining factories,
were infested with hearty muskrats.

we also learned that we could sell
stretched and dried muskrat pelts
for eight dollars apiece
to the old men who worked behind the counter
at our local sporting goods store.

we decided to cash in
on the "rat of the land".

initially, we could only afford
a couple of clamping, leg-hold traps.

this left us with the unsavory job
of clubbing the poor beasts to death
upon discovery of an entangled specimen.

we immediately realized
we may not have had the stomach
to continue on that barbaric route.

but, only my brother had the funds
to purchase the more efficient and humane
conibear traps,
which would cleanly snap the rodent's neck,
much like a giant mouse trap.

i had to stick with the primitive
leg-hold contraptions.

i dutifully labeled the tags on the traps
with my name, telephone number
and trapper's license info
(which i made up, because i
couldn't afford an actual license).

one morning, while setting my traps,
i discovered a burrow near the water's edge,
which i was sure belonged to a mink.

i had no reason to believe this
other than my burning desire
to land the crown jewel of all furred creatures.

i could already see
the looks of disbelief
on the faces of those old curmudgeons
at the sporting goods store,
when i walked in there with my
luxurious mink pelt.

it would probably even start a bidding war.

that evening,
i drifted off to sleep
dreaming of all the things i could do
with that much money...

...i was woken early the next morning
when an irate man called
to say that he had my trap,
and if i wanted it back
i was to come pick it up at his house.

i jumped onto my bike
and anxiously pedaled to the caller's address.

when i arrived,
the angry man was waiting for me
at the edge of his driveway.
he had my leg-hold trap in his hand.

"what the hell were you thinking
placing this so close to a residential area!?"
he shouted.

i responded meekly,
that i was hoping to catch
a mink.

"a MINK?!" he exclaimed,
"are you some kind of moron?
there aren't any mink around here!"

he pointed to his young daughter,
who stood behind him in the driveway,
crying.

in her arms was a sad-looking CAT
with a large cast on its front leg.

"the only thing you managed to catch
was our poor mitzie!"
he proclaimed, in a mocking tone.

upon hearing this,
his daughter sobbed even louder,
milking the situation for
all it was worth.

i looked down, solemnly.

"what i should do is call the
police!" he continued.

at this point,
whether from self-preservation
or actual empathy,
i looked up with tears in my eyes.

the man softened just enough
to reluctantly hand the leg-hold trap back to me.

"well... here's your goddamn trap" he said,
"and don't let me catch you around here again."

i wiped my face and gratefully accepted
the cat-maiming device back from him...

...a few minutes later
as i was biking home,
i looked down at the trap
which was now dangling from my handlebars.

it was caked with blood
and still had a small clump
of fur stuck to it.

i shuddered,
before grasping it and throwing it
into the bushes along the river bank.

then i turned onto sycamore street
and pedaled toward home
as quickly as i could.

sister vincent

sister vincent was raised by
a widower father who worked
long hours in the pennsylvania coal mines
and was an amateur boxer.

during class at saint agnes
she would tell stories
about the thousands of hours she spent
around boxing rings
as a child.

in fact,
much of her youth was spent
in her father's corner,
serving as both his trainer
and cut-man.

she brought that
welterweight mentality
with her to the convent
and eventually,
to saint agnes grammar school.

while disciplining us,
she would often employ "ring speak",
using phrases like:
"saved by the bell",
"pulling your punches" and "out for the count".

her pet peeve
was the long hair
billy flynn and i began to sport
in seventh grade.

she lectured us at great length
about grooming, dress codes
and the tight haircuts
the boxers of her father's generation wore.

sister vincent felt a young man
should be lean and clean,
to assure the best chance
of salvation.

but this was the 1970s
and we were more interested in
looking like jimmy page
than jimmy carter.

eventually,
sister vincent
realized we would not be swayed
by sentiment,
so she turned to shaming.

she began to call us her
"tender contenders"
and proceeded to attack
our masculinity.

each morning she'd have us
sit on top of our desks
with our legs crossed
like a "girl".

then she'd put our hair in barrettes
and spray it with copious amounts
of aqua net hair spray.

we were forced to wear those hairstyles
for the entire school day
under threat of suspension
if we changed them.

one morning,
i attempted to show her
just how little her punishment affected me
by showing up for school
with my hair already coiffed.

i had used the biggest
plastic, daisy barrette i could find
in my sister's dresser drawer
and wore it prominently.

this sent sister vincent into a tizzy.

she stepped toward me
and smacked the side of my head
with such force
it sent the daisy barrette
flying across the classroom.

then she stormed out,
ordering me to
follow her to the principal's office...

...when i arrived,
the principal, sister gosilano
was standing by her desk
as sister vincent paced around the room, fuming.

i tried to appeal to sister gosilano's
latent sense of culture
by noting the important men of history
who wore long locks,
such as
alexander the great, shakespeare,
and benjamin franklin.

when i pointed to the
portrait of jesus hanging
on her office wall
she blew her stack and warned me
not to dare lecture her about the "lord's hair".

she told sister vincent
that she was free to continue
dealing with me however she saw fit,
with immunity.

upon our return to class
sister vincent took extra care
to fix my hair more heinously than ever,
using two barrettes and a
cheerleading squad's worth of hair spray.

then she removed my clip-on tie
and replaced it with one of the cross ties
the girls wore with their uniforms.

she gave me a sinister, satisfied glare
while holding up her index finger.

"round one for the lord,"
she said.

batter up

darryl becker
was older than me,
and so large
that he only needed one hand
to lift my uniformed body over his head
and slam it into a
gasoline-streaked mud puddle
in the little league parking lot.

he used both hands next,
when he took my bike
and threw it on top of me.

then he pinned me down,
pushing against the bicycle with his foot.

he leaned over the puddle
while gripping an aluminum bat
and ordered me to quit the
baseball team,
because i "sucked".

becker didn't have to say
what would happen
if i didn't.

the bat said it all.

it had been his favorite weapon
of torture and intimidation
since the first day i arrived to the field;
undersized and underperforming.

after practice,
he liked to put me in an arm lock,
twisting
until my elbow protruded outward.

then he'd strike the bat against the bone until
i could no longer hold in the tears.

during games,
he'd sit beside me on the bench,
smacking the bat against
the points of my ankles
while calling me a "pussy".

i finally had enough one day
and tendered my resignation to the little league,
even though i knew my father wouldn't tolerate a quitter.

it was number three
on his list of mortal sins,
right behind being
a liar
and a thief.

my father partnered with the coach behind my back
and together they tried to convince me
to stick it out.

during this time,
becker called on the phone,
threatening me to forget about reconsidering,
or next time he would dump me
into the river.

i stuck to my shame
and assured my father that
i would NOT be returning to the team.

i couldn't give him a reason,
because being a coward
was number four on his list
(when paired with quitting, it may have even
leapfrogged to number two).

my humiliation at home
seemed like a small price to pay
in return for not having becker
pummel me three times a week.

plus, he lived
in iroquois heights,
so we weren't likely to
cross paths very often.

over the next few years
i barely thought about darryl becker.

this would end on
my first day of high school,
when everything started up again,
worse than ever.

that morning,
becker saw me sitting at the back
of a double-room study hall.

his eyes locked onto mine
from the front of the room.

he gave me the death stare
and walked the entire length of the room,
slowly and deliberately.

he was savoring my fear.

when he reached the back of the room
he sat next to me
on the side of his chair.

i didn't dare turn toward him,
but i could tell he was
staring a hole through me.

becker didn't say anything
for at least a half minute.

then he stood up
and punched my shoulder
so hard
i fell out of the chair,
spilling my books everywhere
(the resulting bruise didn't fade
for an entire month).

once again,
i couldn't help crying.

and THIS was the point for darryl becker;
while he was ruthlessly violent,
it was only a means to an end.

for him, the real payoff
was witnessing the psychological effect
of tormenting his victims.

he quickly learned my class schedule
and began ambushing me in the hallways.

often times
he would act like he didn't see me coming
until i was within arm's reach,
then he'd dole out
the punishment.

for me,
the hardest part of it all
was that i was already having a
difficult time fitting in
at the public high school,
having transferred from saint agnes.

besides,
this wasn't supposed to be happening to me.

i was in a band.

i actually took some money
i'd made playing at the junior high dance
and tried to solicit
protection
from a few of my larger neighbors
on the south side.

but nobody wanted a piece of becker.

in the end,
i would just have to tough it out
until he graduated,
which he did...with honors.

...i hear today
darryl becker is busy
working as a proctologist;
two hands deep
into someone else's problems.

he also holds
batting practice
every spring
as a little league baseball coach.

buddy

buddy was the most accurately
named dog i've ever met.

he lived next door
with the hinkleys,
but buddy's heart belonged
to all the children of the neighborhood.

he tolerated every bit of love
the kids could give:
extended hugs by two or three children at a time,
funny faces we made with his ears and mouth,
and hundreds of kisses a day
planted all over his
noble head.

buddy was an old retriever
with long, reddish-blond fur
and gentle brown eyes.

his coat was the same color as
the autumn sycamore leaves
that fell from the trees on our street
(often we would walk in front of the hinkley's house,
not noticing buddy lying in the fallen leaves
until he jumped up to greet us).

buddy must have acquired
his big heart and loving temperament
from the family that raised him,
because the hinkleys
were genuinely warm, nurturing people.

one october,
when i was in sixth grade,
they even hired me
to take care of buddy and their fish while
they were on a week-long vacation.

this was a rare gesture,
to put faith in a boy
who was firmly entrenched in a childhood slump.

for this reason,
i went about my duties
as responsibly as i could.

each morning i fed buddy and the fish,
and then let buddy outside.
before leaving for school, i put buddy back in.
this regimen was repeated in the afternoon.

everything was going well
until i came home late one day
to find buddy sleeping at the back door.

i realized i had
forgotten to put him inside that morning
and felt terrible.

i quietly walked onto the porch to give buddy
a hug and apologize,
but when i put my hand on his back
he was as hard as stone
and quite dead.

i burst into tears and ran next door to find my father,
who was already getting a large trash bag ready.

he told me that a neighbor
had seen buddy
lying in the sycamore leaves next to the curb
when a UPS truck pulled up and ran him over,
never seeing him through the leafy camouflage.

apparently,
buddy had dragged himself to the back door,
where he later died.

i was devastated,
but knew it was my responsibility
to call the hinkleys myself
and give them the bad news.

the hinkleys, in their selfless way,
didn't dwell on their own loss.

they only showed concern for my feelings
and whether i was all right.

when they returned,
they brought special gifts for me:
a baseball bat and a batting helmet.

consolation
for the guilty.

the older kids in the neighborhood
picked on me by saying
i should have also killed the fish,
then i would have gotten a new football too.

the younger kids
never said so,
but i knew they held it against me.

seventh heaven

crossing the bridge by our house
led to two places
before continuing out of town:

one was mount seneca,
where every kid from the south side
went for unchaperoned adventure,
and the other was iroquois heights,
which my father referred to as
"snob hob".

nobody from iroquois heights
worked in the factories or labor shops
and their names often had abbreviations attached to them:
starting with dr.
or ending with esq.

most of my friends from saint agnes lived there.

mount seneca's distinction
was being the highest point in the valley
and being covered in dense forest.

at the very peak of mount seneca
was a mythical place
known as
seventh heaven.

we used to listen avidly
as our parents would
reminisce about seventh heaven
over backyard picnic tables.

they spoke of it being an amusement park
when they were kids,
and said you used to be able to see
the ferris wheel lights
from all the way in town.

long before us younger kids
had ever made it up to seventh heaven,
we heard the accounts of older kids
returning from explorations
of weed-covered roller coaster tracks,
rickety fun houses
and rusty bumper cars.

by the time i reached the peak
of mount seneca
i was in fourth grade,
and the legendary seventh heaven
had joined the shuttered factories
on the north end of town
as fossilized skeletons of our city's
glory days.

all that was left
were vestigial, concrete foundations
of ring toss booths
and shooting galleries.

in fact,
seventh heaven had never stopped
being a shooting gallery.

on our first trip to the top
we spent hours exploring the myriad of bullet holes
that had been left in anything solid
by generations of juvenile marksmen.

we put our fingers into every hole
like little doubting thomases,
yet to experience the marvelous power of firearms.

it was a glorious day at
the beginning of sixth grade
when paul verducci walked into saint agnes
and announced that he had received
a pump pellet gun for his birthday.

paul was an awkward blend of
ichabod crane and t.v.'s gilligan,
with a bit of eddie haskell
thrown in for good measure.

he needed a gun like
caesar needed a brutus.

but paul lived in iroquois heights
and there wasn't much he wanted
that he didn't get.

besides, kids from the south side
weren't particular about their paths to mischief...

by first recess
billy flynn and i
had arranged to take paul verducci
and his pump pellet gun
up to seventh heaven for some target practice.

the pump pellet gun
was a revelation
because of the hinged pump on the barrel stock,
which increased its velocity
and made our bb guns seem like pea-shooters.

with 25-30 pumps
the pellet gun would easily kill
any small animal.

we spent the afternoon
on seventh heaven
shooting at anything that moved,
and many things that didn't.

by the end of the afternoon
we had become adept at applying 30-35 pumps
by two of us holding the barrel
while the third worked the pump
with both hands.

before we started our descent
down the mountain,
we decided to pump the gun to its pneumatic limit
in case we encountered a renegade squirrel
or free-spirited sparrow.

on the pathway down,
the lack of live targets and simple juvenile waywardness
led billy into his assumed role of
paul's antagonist.

as billy started throwing acorns at the back of paul's head
and poking sticks into his shoulder blades,
i began to feel like moe
trying to keep larry and curly in line.

it soon became clear to everyone but billy
that paul had finally had enough.

paul turned
and pointed the gun in mock defense
as billy released
one last acorn.

paul dodged to avoid it
and lost his footing on the dirt path...
and the GUN went off!
the silent shock on billy's face
and the tell-tale hole in his pantleg
subtly announced
that the round had hit its mark.

billy slowly slid to the ground
and gasped,
"paul shot me."

despite concern over billy being wounded,
the three of us immediately discussed consequences.

we knew the mishap
would surely lead to the confiscation
of paul's new gun,
so, we agreed to deal with the situation
on our own...

my obsession with my mother's nursing journals
(they often displayed incidental, clinical nudity)
and vast knowledge of t.v. medical procedures
led to my appointment as mountain-top surgeon.

i sent paul home for rags,
tweezers and alcohol,
and helped billy hobble
to an abandoned structure on the hillside,
where i could examine the wound.

as i pressed on the skin above billy's knee
i could see the shiny tip
of the lead pellet
lodged behind his kneecap.

upon paul's return
i poured a capful of alcohol on the hole
and began digging with the tweezers.
after a few minutes of futile exploration,
accented by billy's plaintiff wailing,
we decided to "bite the bullet"
and take him to paul's house
to confess
and seek proper medical attention.

the consequence of our better judgment
would be the affirmation
of our worst fear:

the loss of paul's gun privileges
and our return to fishing poles,
leg-hold traps
and our own side of the river.

ten in the clip

most of the young men in our town had one.
i got mine when i was twelve.

it was a ruger .22 caliber, semi-automatic
with a ten round cartridge
(pre-loading a bullet into the firing chamber
gave me eleven).

by the time i was fifteen
our family arsenal contained a couple of rifles,
three or four shotguns
and my father's .357 magnum.

we were hunters.

we went after small game,
big game,
and thousands of small targets
placed on a big tree
by the pond
at our hunting cabin in the woods.

the big tree eventually gave in
and went down one night.

the light of the following morning
revealed a nearly solid core of lead
where the trunk had snapped.

in our town
young men learned
how to operate guns
long before they even knew
how their dicks worked.

this didn't mix well
with the bleak depression
of a withering factory town.

many teenage boys wore
fluorescent orange
or camouflage hunting gear
year-round
like a uniform.

their badge
was the hunting license
pinned to the back of their jacket.

our high school even had a rifle club
and the school system allowed every student
one legal absence per year for hunting
(not for painting, practicing violin, planting trees or
feeding the homeless... only hunting).

one member of the rifle club
was irving egan;
an under-spoken honor student
who was an alumnus
of saint agnes school.

one afternoon,
during christmas break,
irving took some guns
into the empty high school.

he opened a window
that overlooked the large schoolyard
and the surrounding neighborhood.

he took aim,
and began shooting pedestrians
like they were carnival ducks on a wheel.

when he finally stopped,
he had murdered three people
and wounded eleven others.

one of those killed
was a pregnant woman.

irving committed suicide in his jail cell
by hanging himself with a bed sheet.

this shooting was unique
in a town
where gun violence was mostly
of the self-inflicted variety:

the first time i put a rifle to my head was
during my freshman year of high school.
but i knew it wasn't loaded.

before that,
in junior high,
i sat on the edge of my bed
holding the unloaded gun in both hands
until my fear
was spinning in my chest,
whining like a dentist's drill.

by my sophomore year of high school
i had developed the nerve
to sit there
and hold it
loaded...

ben

they say ben doesn't drink anymore.
but he's already put in his miles.

when i was fourteen or fifteen years old
i began the sacred ritual of
going to ben's house for beer.

my friends had told me many times about
ben's house, ben's stories
and drinking beer with ben.
but this was my first invitation.

i was expecting a middle-aged robert deniro
in a smoking jacket,
with searching eyes
and a brushfire wit.

then i met ben.

ben had the withered visage of a scarecrow
with no front teeth
and a pale, film-cloaked right eye
that had been demolished
by a mop handle when he was in the army.

this happened during a drunken barracks fight
(which also cost him
the aforementioned front teeth).

ben lived in the bottom, back apartment
of a run-down "hotel" that was filled with
old-time pensioners and disabled vets.

the entire place smelled like the one corner of a house
where a cat likes to piss
if you leave it alone for too long.
the walls were painted in a dingy hue
that fell so precisely between blue and green
that its true shade would become our favorite object
of bet and conjecture.

the nightly activities at ben's
(drinking and teen bullshitting)
would take place in his dimly-lit, smoky kitchen
where the cabinets were plastered
with pornographic photos
and clippings of dirty jokes.

i thought that kitchen was the coolest place i'd ever seen.

any night ben could be found
huddled over his kitchen table
drinking beer and straightening the smokeable portions
of crushed cigarette butts.

at ben's
the beer rules were simple:

* you'd buy — he'd fly
(except once a month, when he got his disability check)

* quantity over quality

* no beer left the apartment

and most importantly —
* any unfinished beer was poured
into the pitchers in ben's fridge
for his daytime drinking needs
(pouring "wounded soldiers" into the sink was unforgivable).

it was in ben's kitchen
that my friends and i talked about
conquering the world.

my story
was about becoming a famous musician
who dated the most beautiful women in the world
and spent money freely.

whenever i finished talking about it,
ben would let out a wide-open, throaty laugh
(which would lead into a coughing spasm).

then he would say
that he was gonna know i had hit it big
by the truckload of beer i would send
to his back door.

then ben would smile at me
and wink
with his good eye.

fireball

by junior year of high school,
the daily joints i bought with my lunch money
were failing to create enough headspace
between myself and the world.

so, one friday in october
i decided to up the ante...

my teacher that morning, ms. dayton,
didn't seem to notice much out of the ordinary
until about a half-hour
after the mushrooms kicked in.

i could tell she was on to me then,
as i watched
the streams of orange and purple color
dripping from her hair.

when she finally spoke,
her voice was awash in reverb,
with a pronounced tremolo effect
and the bass distorted.

she sounded like she was underwater,
even though the glowing liquid that was seeping up
through the floorboards
had barely covered our ankles by then.

i glanced around and noticed the other students
diligently toiling away, paying no attention to her,
so i decided to do the same.

i kept my head down
and tried to play it cool,
even though i could hear her
hissing and croaking while standing
right in front of my desk.
when the bell finally rang,
i looked up to see her ruby-red throat
pulsing in and out like a giant bullfrog.

i grabbed my books
and headed for the door
while trudging through the bright liquid,
which was now above my knees.

it disappeared completely
as i entered the hallway and
melted into a sea of students...

...i sauntered into wood shop
later that afternoon, but
our instructor, mr. hanson,
was far more streetwise
than ms. dayton.

he could tell right away that my eyeballs
were still swimming around inside my head,
so, he assigned me to the sign-out sheet
in the tool room.

there, i would pose
the least amount of danger to myself.

once my classmates were busy
working away on cutting boards and bird houses,
i was alone and noticed someone had left
an atomic fireball atop the shelf
of the half-door.

i unwrapped the jawbreaker and studied it,
mesmerized by the brilliant red flames
which began swirling beneath the surface.

i popped it into my mouth
and was seized by a
scorching, cinnamon burst
(undoubtedly multiplied by hallucination).

i opened my jaws to draw a cooling breath
and promptly got the fireball
lodged in my throat.

i panicked, unable to breathe
and clutching my chest as
the nuclear blast flared against my tonsils.

i pounded on the half-door of the shed,
but was drowned-out by the cacophony of
power saws and machinery in the shop.

i became dizzy and fell to my knees,
somehow swallowing the hard candy in the process.

my ears, nose and throat
were a raging volcano
and i couldn't shake the feeling that
the fireball was still stuck
somewhere in my esophagus.

but at least i could breathe again.

eating, however,
would be a different matter.

the experience had left me with
an acute case of
pseudodysphagia,
which, in layman's terms
is the fear of choking.

for the next five weeks
i refused to eat solid food,
instead subsisting on
chicken broth, tomato soup
and ice cream.

since my mother was a nurse,
she arranged for me to come to the hospital
for a complete battery of tests.

then she sat me down with a doctor
who showed me an anatomy book
and assured me that swallowing is
an autonomic function.

out of desperation,
my mother took me to one of
the few therapists in our town who
worked with teenagers.

but he was from iroquois heights
and his stuck-up daughter was in my grade,
so i wasn't gonna talk to that guy
about anything.

besides, he spent the whole
session lecturing me about drugs
and alcohol.

eventually, i confided in the
only person i could trust:
billy flynn.

billy and i theorized that
we should first try to
recreate my mental condition
from that fateful day with the fireball.

then, if i could successfully eat
something solid,
it just might cause a RESET on
that part of my psyche.

a few days later,
we each munched a couple grams of
ground-up liberty caps
on our way to school,
washing them down with a warm pepsi.

we estimated this would put me in
the desired psychedelic state
right around lunchtime.

at noon we rushed to the cafeteria,
where we grabbed some ham and cheese sandwiches
before bolting out to the parking lot.

we found a remote corner
near the wood shop
and unwrapped our lunches.

billy gave me a reassuring nod
as i took a deep breath
and devoured the entire ham and cheese
right then and there.

he gave me half of his sandwich
and i made short work of that as well.

a wave of relief washed over me.

we decided to ditch
the rest of the afternoon
and i headed toward home.

i was even looking forward
to the boiled dinner
my mother was planning for supper that night.

one for the road

it began with finishing the last bit
of my father's beers,
stealing gulps of altar wine after mass,
and mixing together
one pour from each bottle
in my parents' liquor cabinet.

all of my friends
had the same agenda.

before dances at
saint agnes
we would fill mayonnaise jars
with flat beer from the tap
my father installed on an old refrigerator
that sat on our back patio.

in high school,
we would spend our lunch money on loose joints
and a bottle of anything cheap.

we'd blow out school
and head to the river,
where we'd sit under the
bridge by my house
and watch the current race away.

in our town
alcohol was everywhere,
and by the time we were seniors
proximity had led to osmosis.

the students at our school
had a decade-old tradition
called "senior skip weekend".

tickets were sold
for weeks in advance.

$7 would allow you to drink all weekend
from the 30-40 kegs of beer that would be consumed
and would give you a chance to win the raffle prizes:
a gallon of jack daniels
and an ounce of marijuana.

the party was usually held
across the river, at an old, abandoned
schoolhouse in the forest.

at our senior skip weekend
we met a new drinking buddy:
a guy from a neighboring town
who emerged from the woods
and joined the party.

he had a full backpack
and said he had hitchhiked his way there.

most of us brought tents to stay the weekend,
and the hitchhiker set up his tent too.

we all spent three days
drinking, smoking pot
and eating psilocybin mushrooms.

on the closing evening,
the hitchhiker said his good-byes,
gathered his gear
and stumbled toward the forest.

through foggy eyes
i watched him swaying under the weight of his pack,
and the load of his head...

later that year,
i was underage
in a neighborhood bar.

it was 25-cent draft night
and i had already spent a couple bucks.

as i was starting to walk out,
i nearly tripped over a wheelchair
and turned to apologize to the occupant.

it was the hitchhiker
from senior skip weekend.

as we shook hands
i looked down and noticed
his legs had been cut off
above the knees.

i looked up, and knew
that he had caught me staring.

he grabbed hold of my arm by the wrist,
and told me about
the night he left the senior skip party.

he said he had passed out
on the side of the freeway while hitchhiking
and his legs were run over
by a passing truck.

i stood there,
frozen in disbelief.

without letting go of my wrist,
he turned to the bartender
and ordered us each another shot of whiskey.

"one for the road," he said.

the island

the island i grew up on
was a small, catholic valley
surrounded by a thick forest of mountains.

much of the town was bordered by a river
that served as a moat between the hills and the city.

it was a brown, fast moving current
that wasn't waiting.

it was eager to claim those who would bypass
the three bridges that crossed over it.
and sometimes
it did.

the river ran two blocks south of sycamore street.
its huge, grass-covered dikes
were constructed long before i was born.

this project followed a massive flood
in which the river swelled until it had swallowed
half of the city.

i grew up around fading black & white photographs of
houses that looked like they were floating,
and automobiles
half buried in water.

as children playing in the park,
we were warned not to cross to the other side of the dikes
because the river was too fast and dangerous.

as older kids, we were told
not to swim in the river
because of severe, hidden under-currents.

these warnings
were periodically accented
with tragedies:

there was the woman who was a student at the catholic
university on the river's edge.
she drowned during a late night swim.
and there was the high school student
who drowned while trying to escape the police
by breaststroking across its waters.

it seemed that many people
played out their final chapter
in or around that river.

there were accidents,
suicides,
and plenty of general misfortune.

in all,
it was enough to keep me from
ever entering it
during my childhood.

but, i hadn't always feared the river.

my earliest associations of it
were filled with romantic notions of adventure and escape.

as a young boy,
i played with my brother
in the old canoe that rested against the fence
in my grandparents' backyard.

it was in this canoe that my uncle "bear"
had traveled
across the united states, north to south.

he started from the bridge by our house
and continued down the river
until it became the mississippi
and eventually reached the gulf of mexico.

the trip lasted 72 days.

my uncle was nineteen at the time.

years later, as my brother and i played in that canoe,
the front of it still bore the words
"new york — new orleans".

throughout my childhood, i would ask my uncle
about the places he'd been on the river,
the people he'd met,
the mississippi, new orleans
and most of all:
when he was going to take me
on a canoe trip.

he always told me
we would go when i turned sixteen.
and we did.

in the summer of my sixteenth year
three of my uncles took me on a seven day journey
down the river.

one of the boats we took
was the canoe from my grandparents' backyard.

we spent long, hard days rowing
through mountains, forests,
small towns and industrial cities.

in the evenings we set up camp, cooked,
played poker and told stories.
each night,
uncle bear and i
stayed up late around the campfire,
drinking whiskey
and talking about life, family and philosophy.

i returned from that trip
with unprecedented feelings of power,
esteem and purpose.
i knew exactly who i was
and where i was going.

i remember flexing my muscles
in front of the full-length mirror
to see if i looked as transformed as i felt.

even the river seemed less forbidding,
for beyond it
was the entire world...

... this optimism
would be ripped apart
four months later
when my friend, billy flynn
found his exit
on the banks of the river,
by bringing his father's .357 magnum
to his head...

... a year and a half later
i was eighteen.

i stood on the railing
of the bridge by our house
and looked down
at the brown, fast moving current
that wasn't waiting.

then i looked back
at the island.

it was full of motion,
but without
movement.

it was then
that i turned away
and made my own.

elegy for me

good evening father
i have to confess,
i've got no convictions of faith to profess.
but, if you don't mind i'd still like to be blessed.
because i've got tomorrow hanging over me.

acknowledgements:

I would like to thank Marc Estrin and Donna Bister from Fomite Press for guidance in editing, layout and cover design, and for ushering this book into the light of day. Thanks for treating these pieces as poetry, while still calling them stories.

I would like to thank the following people for inspiration and encouragement in writing. First and foremost, to Jamie Chapman, without whom the execution of this book would have never been undertaken. I'd also like to thank Goran Dukic, Amy Johnston, Scott Frank, Jim Krusoe, Renee Brody, Colleen Dunn Bates and Jeff Radt.

Big appreciation and love to my mother, father and siblings for always being there for me. Lastly, I wish to thank my daughter, Harper for allowing me to view childhood through a lens of renewed optimism and faith.

about the author

Bobby Johnston is a Los Angeles based film composer and multi-instrumentalist. "The Saint I Ain't: Stories from Sycamore Street" is his first book.

Fomite

About Fomite

A fomite is a medium capable of transmitting infectious organisms from one individual to another.

"The activity of art is based on the capacity of people to be infected by the feelings of others." Tolstoy, *What Is Art?*

Writing a review on Amazon, Good Reads, Shelfari, Library Thing or other social media sites for readers will help the progress of independent publishing. To submit a review, go to the book page on any of the sites and follow the links for reviews. Books from independent presses rely on reader-to-reader communications.

For more information or to order any of our books, visit:
http://www.fomitepress.com/our-books.html

More Titles from Fomite...

Novels

Joshua Amses — *During This, Our Nadir*
Joshua Amses — *Ghatsr*
Joshua Amses — *Raven or Crow*
Joshua Amses — *The Moment Before an Injury*
Charles Bell — *The Married Land*
Charles Bell — *The Half Gods*
Jaysinh Birjepatel — *Nothing Beside Remains*
Jaysinh Birjepatel — *The Good Muslim of Jackson Heights*
David Brizer — *Victor Rand*
L. M Brown — *Hinterland*
Paula Closson Buck — *Summer on the Cold War Planet*
Dan Chodorkoff — *Loisaida*
Dan Chodorkoff — *Sugaring Down*
David Adams Cleveland — *Time's Betrayal*
Paul Cody— *Sphyxia*
Jaimee Wriston Colbert — *Vanishing Acts*
Roger Coleman — *Skywreck Afternoons*
Marc Estrin — *Hyde*
Marc Estrin — *Kafka's Roach*
Marc Estrin — *Speckled Vanities*
Marc Estrin — *The Annotated Nose*
Zdravka Evtimova — *In the Town of Joy and Peace*
Zdravka Evtimova — *Sinfonia Bulgarica*
Zdravka Evtimova — *You Can Smile on Wednesdays*

Fomite

Daniel Forbes — *Derail This Train Wreck*
Peter Fortunato — *Carnevale*
Greg Guma — *Dons of Time*
Richard Hawley — *The Three Lives of Jonathan Force*
Lamar Herrin — *Father Figure*
Michael Horner — *Damage Control*
Ron Jacobs — *All the Sinners Saints*
Ron Jacobs — *Short Order Frame Up*
Ron Jacobs — *The Co-conspirator's Tale*
Scott Archer Jones — *And Throw Away the Skins*
Scott Archer Jones — *A Rising Tide of People Swept Away*
Julie Justicz — *Degrees of Difficulty*
Maggie Kast — *A Free Unsullied Land*
Darrell Kastin — *Shadowboxing with Bukowski*
Coleen Kearon — *#triggerwarning*
Coleen Kearon — *Feminist on Fire*
Jan English Leary — *Thicker Than Blood*
Diane Lefer — *Confessions of a Carnivore*
Diane Lefer — *Out of Place*
Rob Lenihan — *Born Speaking Lies*
Colin McGinnis — *Roadman*
Douglas W. Milliken — *Our Shadows' Voice*
Ilan Mochari — *Zinsky the Obscure*
Peter Nash — *Parsimony*
Peter Nash — *The Perfection of Things*
George Ovitt — *Stillpoint*
George Ovitt — *Tribunal*
Gregory Papadoyiannis — *The Baby Jazz*
Pelham — *The Walking Poor*
Andy Potok — *My Father's Keeper*
Frederick Ramey — *Comes A Time*
Joseph Rathgeber — *Mixedbloods*
Kathryn Roberts — *Companion Plants*
Robert Rosenberg — *Isles of the Blind*
Fred Russell — *Rafi's World*
Ron Savage — *Voyeur in Tangier*
David Schein — *The Adoption*
Lynn Sloan — *Principles of Navigation*
L.E. Smith — *The Consequence of Gesture*
L.E. Smith — *Travers' Inferno*
L.E. Smith — *Untimely RIPped*

Fomite

Bob Sommer — *A Great Fullness*
Tom Walker — *A Day in the Life*
Susan V. Weiss —*My God, What Have We Done?*
Peter M. Wheelwright — *As It Is On Earth*
Suzie Wizowaty — *The Return of Jason Green*
Poetry
Anna Blackmer — *Hexagrams*
L. Brown — *Loopholes*
Sue D. Burton — *Little Steel*
David Cavanagh— *Cycling in Plato's Cave*
James Connolly — *Picking Up the Bodies*
Greg Delanty — *Loosestrife*
Mason Drukman — *Drawing on Life*
J. C. Ellefson — *Foreign Tales of Exemplum and Woe*
Tina Escaja/Mark Eisner — *Caida Libre/Free Fall*
Anna Faktorovich — *Improvisational Arguments*
Barry Goldensohn — *Snake in the Spine, Wolf in the Heart*
Barry Goldensohn — *The Hundred Yard Dash Man*
Barry Goldensohn — *The Listener Aspires to the Condition of Music*
R. L. Green — *When You Remember Deir Yassin*
Gail Holst-Warhaft — *Lucky Country*
Raymond Luczak — *A Babble of Objects*
Kate Magill — *Roadworthy Creature, Roadworthy Craft*
Tony Magistrale — *Entanglements*
Gary Mesick — *General Discharge*
Andreas Nolte — *Mascha: The Poems of Mascha Kaléko*
Sherry Olson — *Four-Way Stop*
Brett Ortler — *Lessons of the Dead*
David Polk — *Drinking the River*
Janice Miller Potter — *Meanwell*
Janice Miller Potter — *Thoreau's Umbrella*
Philip Ramp — *The Melancholy of a Life as the Joy of Living It Slowly Chills*
Joseph D. Reich — *A Case Study of Werewolves*
Joseph D. Reich — *Connecting the Dots to Shangrila*
Joseph D. Reich — *The Derivation of Cowboys and Indians*
Joseph D. Reich — *The Hole That Runs Through Utopia*
Joseph D. Reich — *The Housing Market*
Kenneth Rosen and Richard Wilson — *Gomorrah*
Fred Rosenblum — *Playing Chicken with an Iron Horse*
Fred Rosenblum — *Vietnumb* \
David Schein — *My Murder and Other Local News*

Fomite

Lawrence Schimel — *Desert Memory: Poems of Jeannette L. Clariond*
Harold Schweizer — *Miriam's Book*
Scott T. Starbuck — *Carbonfish Blues*
Scott T. Starbuck — *Hawk on Wire*
Scott T. Starbuck — *Industrial Oz*
Seth Steinzor — *Among the Lost*
Seth Steinzor — *To Join the Lost*
Susan Thomas — *In the Sadness Museum*
Susan Thomas — *The Empty Notebook Interrogates Itself*
Sharon Webster — *Everyone Lives Here*
Tony Whedon — *The Tres Riches Heures*
Tony Whedon — *The Falkland Quartet*
Claire Zoghb — *Dispatches from Everest*

Poetry - Dual Language
Vito Bonito/Alison Grimaldi Donahue — *Soffiata Via/Blown Away*
Antonello Borra/Blossom Kirschenbaum — *Alfabestiario*
Antonello Borra/Blossom Kirschenbaum — *AlphaBetaBestiaro*
Antonello Borra/Anis Memon — *Fabbrica delle idee/The Factory of Ideas*
Aristea Papalexandrou/Philip Ramp — *Μας προσπερνά/It's Overtaking Us*
Mikis Theodoraksi/Gail Holst-Warhaft — *The House with the Scorpions*
Paolo Valesio/Todd Portnowitz — *La Mezzanotte di Spoleto/Midnight in Spoleto*

Stories
MaryEllen Beveridge — *After the Hunger*
MaryEllen Beveridge — *Permeable Boundaries*
Jay Boyer — *Flight*
L. M Brown — *Treading the Uneven Road*
L. M Brown — *Were We Awake*
Michael Cocchiarale — *Here Is Ware*
Michael Cocchiarale — *Still Time*
Neil Connelly — *In the Wake of Our Vows*
Catherine Zobal Dent — *Unfinished Stories of Girls*
Zdravka Evtimova —*Carts and Other Stories*
John Michael Flynn — *Off to the Next Wherever*
Derek Furr — *Semitones*
Derek Furr — *Suite for Three Voices*
Elizabeth Genovise — *Where There Are Two or More*
Andrei Guriuanu — *Body of Work*
Zeke Jarvis — *In A Family Way*
Arya Jenkins — *Blue Songs in an Open Key*

Fomite

Jan English Leary — *Skating on the Vertical*
Marjorie Maddox — *What She Was Saying*
William Marquess — *Badtime Stories*
William Marquess — *Because Because Because Because Because*
William Marquess — *Boom-shacka-lacka*
William Marquess — *Things I Want You to Do*
Gary Miller — *Museum of the Americas*
Jennifer Anne Moses — *Visiting Hours*
Martin Ott — *Interrogations*
Christopher Peterson — *Amoebic Simulacra*
Christopher Peterson — *Scratch the Itchy Teeth*
Charles Phillips — *Dead South*
Jack Pulaski — *Love's Labours*
Charles Rafferty — *Saturday Night at Magellan's*
Ron Savage — *What We Do For Love*
Fred Skolnik— *Americans and Other Stories*
Lynn Sloan — *This Far Is Not Far Enough*
L.E. Smith — *Views Cost Extra*
Caitlin Hamilton Summie — *To Lay To Rest Our Ghosts*
Susan Thomas — *Among Angelic Orders*
Tom Walker — *Signed Confessions*
Silas Dent Zobal — *The Inconvenience of the Wings*

Odd Birds
Micheal Breiner — *the way none of this happened*
Bill Davis — *Cheap Gestures*
J. C. Ellefson — *Under the Influence: Shouting Out to Walt*
David Ross Gunn — *Cautionary Chronicles*
Andrei Guriuanu & Teknari — *The Darkest City*
Gail Holst-Warhaft — *The Fall of Athens*
Roger Lebovitz — *A Guide to the Western Slopes and the Outlying Area*
Roger Lebovitz — *Twenty-two Instructions for Near Survival*
dug Nap— *Artsy Fartsy*
Delia Bell Robinson — *A Shirtwaist Story*
Peter Schumann — *A Child's Deprimer*
Peter Schumann — *All*
Peter Schumann — *All, Nothing, Nothing at All*
Peter Schumann — *Belligerent & Not So Belligerent Slogans from the Possibilitarian Arsenal*
Peter Schumann — *Bread & Sentences*
Peter Schumann — *Charlotte Salomon*

Fomite

Peter Schumann — *Diagonal Man Theory + Praxis, Volumes One and Two*
Peter Schumann — *Faust 3*
Peter Schumann — *Planet Kasper, Volumes One and Two*
Peter Schumann — *We*

Plays
Stephen Goldberg — *Screwed and Other Plays*
Michele Markarian — *Unborn Children of America*

Essays
William Benton — *Eye Contact: Writing on Art*
Robert Sommer — *Losing Francis: Essays on the Wars at Home*
George Ovitt & Peter Nash — *Trotsky's Sink*